SEANCHAI

Table of Contents

SEANCHAI (*pronounced shan-a-key*) *is a traditional Irish storyteller and custodian of Gaelic folklore, history, and mythology. Originating as highly respected keepers of oral traditions, they passed down tales, genealogies, and local lore from generation to generation.*

Prologue

Night gathered around the campfire as a tribe of Gaelic men sat with their cloaks pulled close against the cold. Wind moved through the grass beyond the firelight, carrying the scent of peat grass and earth. Above them, the sky stretched wide and endless, stars scattered like embers across the black stone of space. One man rose, carried a log to the fire, and cast it into the dying flames. Sparks lept upward, spiraling into the night, and for a moment it was impossible to tell where the fire ended and heaven began. The seanchaí lifted his voice and spoke these words.

"I fairsinge chosmach, nochtar réaltaí, cogarnaíonn ár bhfórsa beatha, rúin gan insint. Braon deannaigh réalta, agus lasann muid uile i ndamhsa ag caochadh, i solas neamhaí agus i fairsinge gan teorainn; níl ionainn ach cuid atá ceangailte leis an bhfabraic chomh mór sin. Cruinne istigh ionainn, agus cruinne in aice láimhe."

Silenced followed, nobody spoke. Each man held the words in his own way, turning them over their minds like stones in a hand. At last, the seanchaí broke the silence and said, " Long ago, when the world was old and had begun again, there was a cavern deep into a mountain, with a waterfall hiding it from the world, where the first man and woman lived.

The air inside the cavern was heavy with the scent of earth and the slow breath of a dying fire. Shadows clung to the stone walls like memories that refused to fade. Eve's hand had left paintings of trees, birds of all kinds, the sun, and memories of their lives together. She used ochre and charcoal from the fires, telling stories of their days and their dreams. Seen by the flickering of the torchlights that hung unevenly along the rough surfaces. The worn leather of bear skins lay spread out across the cold stone floor. Near the back, a rustic wooden table bore the marks of time. It was scarred and stained from the countless meals shared.

Adam, the first man, lay upon a bed of woven reeds and animal skins. His body was frail and stretched out. His eyes clouded with the long years of the world's sorrow and wonders. His hair and beard were long and unkept. The weight of nine centuries pressed upon his chest: each breath a labor between this life and the next. Beside him, his wife Eve kept silent vigil, holding his hand and thinking about their lives together.

At the foot of his bed stood 308-year-old Enoch, a tall man as well, long hair and a beard, which was custom for that time, marked him as Adam's great-grandson's son. A righteous man, who was told by an angel of Adam's condition, had rushed to be there. On the other side, a young scribe knelt, the last of those who would hear the first man speak. His hand trembled above the parchment, waiting.

Then Adam's voice came as a whisper, rough as the wind that once moved across the garden. "Write what I tell you, "He said. "For these are not my words alone, but the memories of God spoken through the dust." Then the scribe dipped his reed into the ink made from ash and oil, and the cavern was filled with the soft scratching of history being born again.

There is a race of beings; Adam began. Who dwells in a perfect realm, a society of light and harmony. Their leader is called Yahweh, the Father of creation, and his mate is called Asherah, the mother, and their son is called the Prince of Peace. Their kingdom is so magnificent, so splendid that even looking upon it would leave one breathless. I was told that it shines with the Glory of God, its radiance is like a most rare jewel, like a jasper, and clear as a crystal.

It had a great, high wall, with twelve gates, and there was one who had a measuring rod of gold to measure the city and its gates and its walls. The city lies foursquare; its length, width, and height are equal. The walls were built of jasper, while the city was pure gold, like clear water. The foundations of the wall of the city were adorned with twelve kinds of jewels. Each one has a note in the song of creation. The twelve gates were twelve pearls, each of the gates made of a single pearl, and the streets of the city were pure gold. Yahweh rules that city with such wisdom that peace is eternal and alive.

Here on earth, long before I was shaped from the dust, Adam said, "There were seven kingdoms ruled by the others that came from beyond the stars. The greatest of these cities was Atlantis, a great city by the sea, but war broke out between them, over dirt & rock and the jewels that lay beneath the dust. The sky was filled with chariots of fire. These cities saw great destruction, and Father was saddened by it. Adam pauses for a moment and asks for some water. "Greed is a terrible thing; suffered were the women and children," said Adam

However, throughout Father's kingdom, beautiful music fills the air-voices lifted in eternal praise to the Father, the mother, and the Son. These great choirs were led by one being, who was known as the Morning Star, the fairest of them all; some even called him the Shining One. His aura was so bright you could barely look upon him. Yahweh could see the splendor and how others loved him, so he decided that he would put him to the test. He allowed the Morning Star to be corrupted with what I believe was pride.

Suddenly, the Morning Star began to covet praise for his talents and gladly received the worship given to him by others. He then could see how easy it was for him to persuade others with his music and melodies. The more he sought after worship, the more praise he got until the thought entered his mind that he could rise above Yahweh and that he could rule. He traveled throughout the kingdom, convincing one-third of its population to follow him, and a rebellion broke out. However, it was very short-lived because he was not strong enough to defeat Yahweh, and he was utterly defeated.

As punishment for his treachery, he was banished from the kingdom and thrown down to a nearby planet, and he and his followers collided with the surface of that planet so hard that it destroyed every living thing. Before that horrific day, the inhabitants lived on a planet that was a vibrant, thriving planet, teeming with life. Towering trees stretched towards the sky, their leaves rustling in the gentle breeze. Rivers flowed with crystal clear water, home to an array of aquatic life. The air was filled with the sweet songs of birds and the roars of majestic creatures that roamed the land. The inhabitants walked alongside these creatures, living in balance with nature. They were a curious species, exploring the world around them and marveling at its beauty. They lived in harmony with one another, their hearts free from malice and deceit. But this world was not to last. The earth was ravaged; its inhabitants were wiped out in an instant.

Even the dinosaurs that walked upon the earth, and those that flew in the sky and swam in the waters, everything, even the plants died, and, in the end, there was only darkness. Lucifer and his fallen angels are flying around, screaming and moaning in agony and torment. The once celestial beings are now trapped on a dead planet. Trapped in darkness and silence except for the pains of anguish from being separated from their home, from their God, all of it was replaced with hatred and vengeance. The Morning Star gathered all together and declared that he would lead them into a new kingdom. They all bowed their knees and swore allegiance to THE RULER OF THE NEW WORLD.

Creation

Then, like a burst of light in the darkness, they heard let there be light, and the light exploded forth, and Father saw that the light was good, and he divided the light from the darkness, and the light he called day and the darkness he called night. However, the Fallen Ones feared the light and hid from it, for in the darkness they could hide their shame.

Then Yahweh said, Let the waters be gathered unto one place and let the dry land appear; and it was so. He called the dry land earth, and the gathered water called Seas; and he saw that it was good. He then said let the earth bring forth grass, the herb yielding seed after his kind, and the tree yielding fruit, whose seed was in itself, upon the earth, and it was so. Then Yahweh said, Let the waters bring forth abundantly the moving creature that hath life, and fowl that may fly above the earth in the open sky. Then he created great whales and every living creature that moved, which the waters brought forth abundantly, after their kind, and every winged fowl after his kind, and he saw that it was good.

Then Yahweh said, "Let us make man in our own image, after our likeness." So, then Yahweh created man in his image and created females in Asherah's image. He then blessed them and said," Be fruitful and multiply and replenish the earth, and subdue it. You have dominion over the fish of the sea and over the fowl of the air, and over every living thing that moves upon the earth. Then he put inside man a deep desire for a woman that he could not quench. He created them, male and female, with a love and intimacy that reflected his own relationship with Asherah.

Morning Star and his followers watched as God created humanity. They saw the awe and beauty of the first humans, and they knew that humans were meant to be a part of this world, but they were the fallen ones. It was all for them, and as humans grew and multiplied. Morning Star and his followers watched with growing resentment. They could see the divinity in Yahweh's creations, the love and affection that humans showed one another, and they remembered the love and worship they had once shown to Yahweh. They began to feel jealous and bitter, and they started to plot against humanity itself.

The Morning Star, once a beautiful and radiant being, began to feel his heart growing even colder and darker. He saw the happiness and unity of humans, and he resented it. He wanted to destroy it, to take away the most important thing that Yahweh had created.

MorningStar and his followers were no more than a mist to these mortals against these ground dwellers, but they had great influence over them and controlled them with just a whisper or a thought. They would appear to them as gods, and men would bow the knee and worship them as gods.

Adam & Eve

One day, Yahweh saw how the Shining One had corrupted his creation and would rule over them as if he were a god, so Father and Mother decided to create a man in his own image. So, he carved me out of the dirt and minerals in the ground and then breathed life into me. He watched as the clay transformed into skin, soft and vulnerable, followed by bones that hardened into strength. Tendons and muscles appeared beneath my skin. Hair sprouted from my scalp, dark and wild, and I was over fifteen feet tall, a giant of a man. Then Asherah spoke that I needed a help mate, thank you Asherah for that, she said I needed a partner, one that would love me and support me, and give me children, and I had no idea what that would involve so Yahweh removed a rib from me and created a woman in the image of Asherah to be the my helper and partner. Then Asherah stepped forward and breathed into the woman, giving her very essence and everything it was to be a woman, and named her Eve. God then set us apart in a perfect spot where we had everything we would ever need. It was called the Garden of Eden.

It was all ours; we could have everything we wanted, except for one thing—the forbidden fruit of a single tree we were not allowed to eat from. It was a beautiful tree, filled with tempting, luscious fruit, the most splendid tree in all the valley. Yahweh called it the Tree of Knowledge of Good and Evil, and He warned us both that if we ever ate from that tree, we would surely die.

"Eve, my darling wife," Adam said as he squeezed her hand. Drawn to undiscovered things, she went to visit the Tree of Knowledge, and that is when she came upon the Shining One, disguised as a snake that could talk.

You see, during this time and in that place of protection, we had dominion over all the creatures. We named them all and could communicate with them. The Shining One used his powers of persuasion, much like he did with those he convinced to follow him and rise up against Yahweh. Eve was no match for such a cunning adversary.

"Did He actually mean that you would die? Surely not. Look how beautiful this fruit is. I bet it tastes even sweeter," the Shining One said.

So, she plucked the fruit from the tree, and she did eat, and it was sweet to her lips, and she knew immediately Good & Evil, and she rebuked the snake, and having accomplished his task, he did leave her. For the first time, fear came upon her, and she didn't know what to do. She sat under the very same tree and devised a plan; she would convince me to partake, and then surely Yahweh wouldn't punish both of us.

So here I came, looking for Eve, and I came upon her under the tree, and I just knew that she was distraught. I came to her, and she convinced me to eat the forbidden fruit, and then instantly I knew Good & Evil. A thousand things were going through my mind, but I couldn't concentrate on them because of Eve. It was like seeing her really for the first time. I saw her beauty, the sparkle of her eyes, and the warmth of her smile. I saw the curves of her body and felt the softness of her skin.

I was drawn to her with a feeling that I had never felt before. You see, when I ate of that fruit, I was then subject to all the emotions and the commandment that God made of man to be fruitful and multiply. I could not control the desire that God put in all men to reproduce. I began to caress Eve, and she, with her hands, began to explore me, and as the animals do, we did for hours; we mated with each other. Then, suddenly, a voice calls out, it was Yahweh who had come down to the valley, and he was looking for us. In a panic, we began to look for something to cover up, perhaps some large leaves or something. Yahweh came to us and asked why did you not answer when I called? Then I replied because we were naked.

Immediately, Yahweh asked who told you that you were naked? Already knowing what we had done, he then asked, "Have you eaten from the tree that I told you not to?" Well, I spoke up and said, "It's this woman that you gave me, she ate it first, it was her fault she did it".

So, Yahweh banished us from that perfect spot and told us it was time for us to move on and experience how life really was. He told me that I was going to have to work hard in the field to provide, which was now my job. To be a hunter and a gatherer to provide. However, as soon as he spoke those words my mind was filled with knowledge on how to do those things. He told Eve that now she would bear offspring just like the animals, and it would be painful. The most painful experience she could ever imagine, and so we went forth hand in hand. Discovering a new land and a new world together. It wasn't long before we found a perfect spot. It was a deep cave with a waterfall in front of it that had provided a place for us, and we planted seeds and watched them grow. Now I know the animals, believe me, I knew which ones were good for eating and which ones to stay away from. Come early fall, we reaped our harvest, and the harvest was plentiful, and Eve became with child.

We Chose To Be Born

So Yahweh commanded that when our child was conceived, He would send His Spirit and create life, so that humankind would be three parts: one part body, one part soul, and one part spirit. And Asherah herself was there to help Eve give birth to Cain, who came forth weighing every bit of ten pounds, with a full head of dark, curly hair.

When Eve saw him, she said, "I have gained a man with the Lord's help," referring to the angel who acted as a midwife. So she named him Cain, which in Hebrew means acquired possession.

Then Yahweh commanded that this happen within all humans conceived from this day forward, from the first to the last. That all who are born shall be three parts: body, soul, and spirit. To be fair and to be just, He allowed His host of angels to volunteer. They would volunteer to leave the comfort of their utopia and be born on earth to live as a man, to be tempted, and tested, to be given the choice of whom to serve—light or darkness, good versus evil. They sacrificed it all for the opportunity to become Children of God. So, then man is without excuse; he cannot say that he didn't choose this life. For it is written that in this life we don't see things as they are, but after death, we see things clearly.

The seanchaí stopped speaking, stood up, threw another log on the fire, and then took a deep breath and said these words:

"I believe we left paradise to be born as humans and to be tried and tested just like the Prince of Peace. By His death came forgiveness of our sins, and with His resurrection came a promise of a return to paradise. As He said to the thief on the cross who believed in Him, 'Today you will be with me in paradise.' All we have to do is believe that He is, that He died on the cross for our sins, and that

He was resurrected on the Third Day, taking the keys to death, hell, and the grave. For we must believe in our hearts and confess with our mouths that Jesus Christ is Lord. Then we must love Yahweh with all our heart, soul, and strength, and the next commandment is to love our brother, our neighbor, the stranger, more than we love ourselves—to help our brothers and sisters return to paradise. For whoever finds his life in this place will surely lose it, but whoever loses his life here in this place for God's sake will surely find his life again in paradise."

Cain & Abel

So Adam continued: we were proud parents, and we learned how to nurture and protect our baby—teaching him how to crawl, take his first steps, and communicate. From the time he was little, he would go hunting with me and help me in the fields with the crops. He loved getting his hands dirty and the coolness of freshly turned soil.

Soon, Mother Eve was pregnant again, and Cain would have a little brother. Once again, Asherah was there to help Eve, and after much pain and turmoil, she delivered another boy. He was fairer than Cain, with light-colored hair and blue eyes. Abel barely weighed six pounds. He was so little and light to Eve that she named him Abel, which means breath or vapor.

Time went by, and both boys grew strong and true. They grew up like most boys do—running and playing in the tall grass, climbing trees, and venturing into dangerous heights. I taught Cain everything I knew about working the fields, the soil, and how to make things grow. Abel's duty was to tend the sheep, keeping them together and fed.

One day, as they were taught by their mother and me, they brought offerings to Yahweh. Cain brought some of his biggest and finest vegetables, while Abel sacrificed the best lamb from his flock, bringing perfect portions of meat. God was pleased with Abel's sacrifice, knowing how deeply he loved his sheep, and thus He rejected Cain.

This angered Cain, and he struggled to control his emotions. His mother and I did not know what to do, and even God Himself tried to reason with him. Yet to Cain, it always seemed as though Abel was favored.

"I was the firstborn son," he would say, his jealousy raging. "I work hard in the fields, breaking my back—and for what? All he does is play with the sheep all day."

Yahweh even tried to console him, telling him that if he did good, he would reap good things. But if he did not, sin—like a tiger—was crouching and ready to pounce.

However, Cain wasn't hearing it, and he invited Abel to go for a walk with him out to the fields. Come on, brother, let's go for a walk, he would say. Abel, sensing something was wrong, tried to console his brother. He would tell him that it didn't mean anything, and maybe the next time, but Cain wasn't hearing it, and he picked up a rock, and he bashed Abel over the head. Abel fell to the ground, and Cain kept striking him. Cain would strike him over and over again, cracking his head wide open. Abel's blood flowed into the once plowed ground.

Now Cain, to cover up what he had done, took Abel's body to an exceedingly high place and threw it down from there. He thought that later, when we went to look for him, he would lead us this way, and we would find him there, making it appear as though he had accidentally fallen from the edge.

Then Cain went to the river and bathed. As he walked home, rehearsing his story to himself, Yahweh appeared and asked him, "Where is Abel?" Cain gave no answer. Yahweh knew what had happened, but He was giving Cain a chance to confess and repent—still, there was no response.

"Cain," the Lord said, "where is your brother?"

Cain replied angrily, "I don't know. Am I my brother's keeper?"

Yahweh looked at Cain dead in the eyes and said, "Cain, your brother's blood cries out to me from the ground."

"I don't know what you're talking about," Cain replied.

"You have to leave this place," Yahweh answered. "I can no longer look upon you; sin has crept into your heart, and love no longer resides there."

As Yahweh walked away, he mumbled, "Now I got to go tell your mother & father what you have done and what you have forced me to do."

Suddenly, Cain yelled, "You can't send me out there! Those people will kill me."

Yahweh turned and faced Cain and said, "You're right."

"No, Lord, please!" responded Cain.

"Very well," Yahweh responded, "I'll place my mark upon you."

(Now, in case you didn't know, God's mark that he put on Cain is the Trinity Knot.)

"For all that sees my mark, no harm should come upon you," said God.

So then Cain did leave his land and his home and wandered into the land of Nod, where he met his wife from the land of Nod, settled down outside of the city, and he never had fellowship with God again.

(Yahweh's mark that he put on Cain ensured no harm came upon him. Yahweh had shown Himself to the others and tried to help them see a better way. What they called miracles were truly acts of God, and upon Yahweh's breastplate, He bore that mark to represent the Trinity. The mark became known far and wide. Those who bore that mark did great things and demonstrated powers never seen before. People were healed from fatal injuries, the lame could walk, and the blind were made to see. The mark represented the Father, the Son, and the Holy Spirit—the Three in One.)

The Watchers

In those days, God sent forth a group of angels—two hundred of them. He sent them throughout the ancient earth to watch over mankind, and those angels were called Watchers. They were charged with protecting humans against the Others, from beyond the stars, should they ever return.

However, Lucifer (the Morning Star) set about deceiving them. He went to the leader, Azazel, and took him to exceedingly high places, showing him the riches of the kingdoms and the allure of human women.

He convinced them that they could live like gods if they would only bow down and worship him. One after another fell to Lucifer's deceptions. They took human women into their beds and mated with them, and their offspring became giants in the land—taller and stronger than any man.

The Watchers took what they wanted: kingdoms and the lands they were on. To gain mankind's loyalty and manipulate them, the Watchers shared secrets of warfare, showing them how to make weapons and use alien technology. They were fruitful and multiplied, and soon they had spread all over the ancient world.

The Watchers showed men all manner of things that God Himself did not want man to know. There were 200 Watchers who had turned and betrayed the will of God. They were scattered across the ancient world, teaching men how to make instruments of war and how to use the healing properties of plants and herbs, as well as how to use dark magic. Soon they started experimenting with animals and humans. They created their labs in their vessels. They took the upper body of a man and the lower body of a bull; it was called a Minotaur. Then they would put the head of a woman on the body of a lion. Then they put the body of a man and the head of a jackal, which was called Anubis. Two hundred Watchers each made two crossbreeds to show their divinity. They crossed humans with animals, and animals with birds, and all things great and small.

However, these were all abominations before God. They took many wives and women and produced many children, which were called Nephilim. They even did worse: they would take different roots and herbs and have the mother take the mixture while pregnant, and it created monsters that outgrew the giants. They ruled with abominations and with fear throughout the ancient world. It was dark times for the humanity of the ancient world, dark times indeed. There were giants and monsters in the land.

Meanwhile, in the land of Nod, Cain settled in a village called Nod Haven, where he met a woman named Azura. She was drawing water from a well, and he had been walking for days. Immediately, Azura knew that he was a stranger in a strange land. She spoke to him and said, "You're a son of Adam," she said.

Cain responded, "Yes, I am. How did you know?"

"You are not like us, for you are different—much taller, and you carry the mark of Yahweh on your forehead. I've heard about your people all of my life, how there was a barrier protecting us from you."

Then Cain saw an opportunity to use her kindness to his advantage. He wooed her with his charm and deceit, eventually gaining her trust and making her his mate.

As Cain's influence grew, he began to manipulate the villagers, using his charisma and intelligence to turn them against each other. He promised them protection and prosperity but delivered only oppression and exploitation. He took control of the village's resources, amassing wealth and power for himself. Cain's rule was marked by fear and intimidation. He used violence and coercion to maintain his grip on power, crushing any opposition and silencing dissenting voices. The villagers lived in terror of him, and his reputation as a ruthless leader spread throughout the land.

Despite his cruel nature, Cain was a cunning strategist, and he knew how to present himself as a benevolent leader. He built grand structures and monuments, claiming they were for the benefit of the people, but in reality, they were testaments to his own power and Glory.

As time passed, Cain's descendants inherited his legacy of power and manipulation. They continued to rule with an iron fist, expanding their dominion over neighboring villages and cities. The people lived in fear of the Cainites, whispering stories of their cruelty and brutality in hushed tones. Cain's story in the land of Nod serves as a cautionary tale about the dangers of unchecked power and the corrupting influence of ambition. Despite his notorious past, Cain was able to reinvent himself as a leader, using his intelligence and charm to manipulate others and achieve his goals.

In the land of Nod, Cain's reputation as a cunning and ruthless leader had reached the attention of the Watchers. These fallen angels, who had been cast out of heaven for their transgressions, saw potential in Cain and decided to contact him.

The Watchers, led by Azazel, approached Cain with offers of knowledge and power. They revealed to him the secrets of metallurgy, showing him how to forge swords, spears, and other instruments of war. Cain, ever eager to increase his power and control, was quick to learn and apply these new skills. With the Watchers' guidance, Cain's arsenal grew, and his military prowess became unmatched. He used his newfound abilities to expand his dominion, conquering neighboring villages and cities.

The people trembled at the sight of Cain's armies, armed with the finest weapons the Watchers had taught him to craft. As Cain's power grew, so did his dependence on the Watchers. He became increasingly entwined with them, relying on their counsel and guidance. The collaboration between Cain and the Watchers had far-reaching consequences. The people of the land lived in fear of Cain's armies, and the sound of clashing steel echoed through the valleys.

The Watchers' influence had unleashed a new era of violence and bloodshed, and Cain was their instrument of destruction. Cain's armies, armed with forged swords and spears, clashed with a coalition of neighboring cities. The battle was fierce, but Cain's forces emerged victorious, thanks to the Watchers' strategic guidance. Cain's armies besieged the city of Han, which was known for its strong walls and defenses. The Watchers taught Cain how to build siege engines and catapults, which allowed him to breach the city's defenses and claim it as a vassal state. These battles cemented Cain's reputation as a powerful and feared leader, and his alliance with the Watchers made him nearly unbeatable in combat. Cain amassed a vast fortune.

He plundered the riches of the cities he conquered, taking gold, silver, and precious gems for himself. The Watchers, in turn, demanded a share of the spoils, but Cain was happy to oblige, knowing that their support was crucial to his continued success. He took many prisoners of war, whom he forced into slavery, and seized large herds of livestock, which he used to build his own wealth and power. The cities that Cain conquered were forced to pay him tribute, which further increased his wealth and influence. Cain's control of key trade routes and his alliance with the Watchers allowed him to dominate the regional economy, amassing wealth through trade and commerce.

As the Cainites continued to multiply and spread, their population grew rapidly. Cain's descendants became skilled in various arts and crafts, such as metalwork, music, and agriculture. However, their talents and abilities were often used for selfish and wicked purposes. The Cainites' wickedness grew as they became more and more entrenched in their sinful ways. They began to disregard God's laws and commands, indulging in immoral behavior and violence. Their cities became hubs of corruption and depravity, with the Cainites engaging in all manner of wickedness.

The sacred letters describes the Cainites as being characterized by their violence, corruption, and arrogance. They were a people who rejected God's authority and lived according to their own desires, without regard for morality or consequences. As the Cainites' population grew, so did their influence. They began to dominate the surrounding regions, spreading their wickedness and corruption to other people. Their presence had a corrupting influence on the ancient world, contributing to the overall decline of humanity's moral and spiritual state. The Cainites' wickedness ultimately contributed to God's judgment on humanity, as described in the biblical account of the flood. Their corruption and violence helped to fill the earth with wickedness, paving the way for God's righteous judgment.

Seth

So, Cain was banished, and Abel was dead. I was deeply troubled, being that I had no son. I was now 130 years old and wondered who would carry the mantle—the relationship with Yahweh. Then one night, I saw Eve smile. She hadn't smiled like that since before we lost Abel, and once again, I knew my wife, who was also 130 years old, had borne me another son… saying, "God has granted me another child in place of Abel, and his name is Seth," which means appointed.

However, this time Asherah wasn't there to help, for the last time she had told me that it would be my duty the next time. So, I had to deliver Seth into this world. I had never heard Eve scream in pain so much, but that boy represents hope and continuity in the lineage. Seth's lineage is significant as it leads to Noah and ultimately the Christ. Now, not knowing if this would be my last chance, I poured myself into Seth. I started teaching him right from wrong even before he could walk, introducing him to different animals and teaching him their purpose and the whole circle of life. As he grew older, I would teach him about God the Father, or by his nickname, Yahweh.

I taught him that He made everything and that without God there would be nothing made. That this place would still be covered in darkness, and nothing would be alive, not even him or his mother. Seth, being a young man, asked me one day, "What was Eden like before the sin? I've heard the stories, but was it truly perfect?"

I paused and looked away from Eve with shame and sadness in my eyes. "Yes, son," I replied. "It was perfect—no death, no suffering, only beauty and God's presence everywhere."

Seth's curiosity grew. "And you played with the lions and bears? Weren't you afraid?"

I kind of smiled. "No, son. There was no fear in Eden. We lived in harmony until we disobeyed God."

Seth's expression turned thoughtful. "So your disobedience broke that harmony?" Thinking of the times that he himself disobeyed his mother, he asked, "Is that why God kicked you out of Eden?"

I nodded my head slowly. "Yes, son. Our sin separated us from God's perfect world. But God promised a way back through our own lineage."

"Father?" Seth replied. "What do you mean?"

"Well," I replied, "It is said that a man will be born in our family that will bruise his heel on the head of the serpent. You know that lying snake that confused your mother. Son, it falls on you and your descendants. Since Cain was cursed and Abel's life was cut short, it is you who will produce a righteous man that will crush the serpent's head, and the serpent will bruise his heel."

Seth looked up at me, determination burning in his eyes. "Father, I'll make sure our family honors God. I'll teach my children and their children to obey Him, so we can right the wrong done to our family and fulfill God's promise!"

I smiled, hope renewed in my eyes. I embraced Seth tightly, tears of joy in my eyes. "I know that you will, son," I whispered, my voice trembling with emotion. Seth felt a surge of love and responsibility. As I pulled back, my eyes sparkled with tears. "You'll restore our family's honor, and God will bless your efforts." Seth then nodded solemnly, his heart filled with determination.

It wasn't long before Seth was leading the family's devotions and showing godly wisdom. People started calling him Seth, son of Adam, servant of God. The day came when Seth decided to right a family wrong and visit his older brother Cain.

A servant announced to Cain that someone proclaiming to be his brother requested an audience with him. Cain, confounded for a moment, thought about Abel: "Could he have survived, or maybe God had resurrected him?"

"Yes, see him in," commanded Cain. Then in walked Seth, his younger brother, whom he had never seen. However, he knew instantly by his physical and facial features that he was a son of Adam, his brother. Cain was a tall and strong man, hairy like a beast, but Seth was more like his brother Abel—a modest-sized man with fair skin.

"Brother, thank you for seeing me with no invitation."

"Anytime," replied Cain. "Anytime. What can I do for you?"

As Seth gazed into Cain's eyes, he noticed the same intensity that drove his brother to commit the unthinkable. He saw strength, power, and unyielding determination, but he also sensed something else—a deep-seated pain, a festering wound that refused to heal.

Seth wondered if Cain's actions were motivated by jealousy, insecurity, or a desire for recognition of all his hard work in the fields—or did the devil simply influence him, as mother and father said? Seth was wary of Cain's power and influence. He knew that his brother's presence could be toxic, and he didn't want to get drawn into his web of darkness.

As Cain gazed at Seth, he was struck by his brother's softness and weakness. He remembered the brother he had killed—the one he thought was favored more by God. He recalled the jealousy that burned within him, the sense of injustice that fueled his rage. But now, looking at Seth, he felt nothing: no anger, no resentment, just a hollow emptiness. He was actually surprised by how little he felt. Cain's mind wandered to the mark on his forehead, the symbol of God's judgment. He wondered what Seth thought of it—if he saw it as a sign of weakness or a reminder of his transgression.

"Well, brother, mother has asked about you and would like for you to come visit her soon. You know how she can be," stated Seth.

Cain, clearing his throat, replied, "Yes, I do."

"How's father?" Cain asked.

"He's well, and they both miss you terribly," said Seth. "Brother, they hold no ill will for you, and they understand failing and not being able to live up to what is expected of you. Why don't you come home and let's be a family again?" Seth asked.

Cain, almost laughing, replied, "You don't know what you're asking. Besides, that God of yours has no mercy for the likes of me."

"You're wrong, brother. It's because of His mercy that you are still living and breathing, and that mark that He has put upon you has gained you favor with the earth's people."

"Rubbish," cried out Cain. "I don't have favor with these earth people. They obey me because they fear me. Come on, brother, father would love to see you."

Cain's eyes narrowed slightly as Seth spoke, his expression unreadable. "I'm not sure I can ever go back, Seth," Cain said, his voice low and measured. "The things I've done and the people I've hurt… I just don't think that I could face mother with that."

Seth's eyes filled with compassion. "They love you, Cain. You're their firstborn. They've always loved you, and God's mercy is greater than any wrong that we have done."

Cain snorted, a bitter smile twisting his lips. "You really believe that, don't you? That God's mercy is enough to wipe away everything I've done?"

Seth nodded, his voice filled with conviction. "Yes, I do, and I think that you need to hear it from someone who cares about you—your father."

Cain's gaze lingered on Seth's face, searching for any sign of insincerity, but all he saw was genuine concern and compassion. Changing the subject, Cain replied, "Come, brother, let me show you my kingdom. Take a walk with me."

"Oh no," Seth answered. "I know what happens to brothers that take walks with you."

Cain, stunned at first, then laughed. "Come on, brother, you'll be okay."

Seth laughed along with his brother and agreed.

Cain proudly showed Seth all that he had, and it really was impressive. But at the end of the day, Seth was discouraged because he had such high hopes of reuniting his family. Time went by, and not much more effort was made. Seth grew old and had children, and then they had children, and life continued until his grandson Jared had a boy named Enoch.

There was something special about that boy. He was the cutest child, and everybody loved him. Enoch never met a stranger. Everybody knew that Enoch was highly favored by Yahweh. From an early age, Enoch demonstrated his knowledge and faith in God.

As a boy, he would pass on the truths that he learned, and even as a child, he spoke with authority and with such wisdom. People were amazed at the commonsense stories he would tell—stories of hope and inspiration.

"God," he would say, "is everywhere. He is in the air that we breathe, in the water that we drink, and in the meat that we eat. Everything was made by God, and without God, there would be nothing made. Before God, this place was dark and void of life."

He commanded that there be light, and then there was light. Then he created the seed that grew into a tree and produced its own seed. Then it fell to the ground and died in the soil. In due time, it came to life, grew up from the soil, and became a tree. He created the worm that crawled on the ground, which went to sleep and woke up with the ability to fly.

Young Enoch explained how God created the animals, male and female, and how they reproduced and made more. He explained how He created the large ones and the very small ones, and how each had a purpose for living.

"Just like us," young Enoch would say. He grew up in hard times. Evil ran roughshod over the people of the earth. There were giants and monsters in the land.

City of Enoch

Enoch was born when his father, Jared, was 162 years old and lived during a time of great wickedness on the earth, yet his life stood out for its righteousness. When Enoch was 65 years old, he became the father of Methuselah, who lived for 969 years. God called Enoch to preach repentance: "Repent, for the Kingdom of Heaven is at hand." Enoch preached repentance to all the people except the Canaanites, for God had already turned them over to a reprobate mind because of their wickedness.

In prayer one day, many years later, Enoch, being an old man, had a vision. Enoch saw the world sinking into utter wickedness, with the Morning Star holding a great chain in his hand. The chain covered the face of the earth with darkness, and he looked up and laughed, and his angels rejoiced. He saw Yahweh in Heaven weeping as He looked upon the wickedness of the world. This was the vision of Enoch.

The name of Enoch spread across the ancient world. People would come for miles to listen to him preach about repentance and to learn of the one true God. Many of them did not want to leave, so they started building houses, temples, and marketplaces, and a city on a hill arose. The city of Enoch was called Zion. It was built on a hill at the base of a mountain called Mount Hermon. The city was protected by white stone walls with towers and massive gates. Due to Enoch's preaching and teaching, the people of the city of Enoch were so righteous that Yahweh Himself would come down and walk along with His people. Enoch would walk with God and talk to Him face to face.

The citizens of the city of Enoch were not limited to one group or one tribe. Enoch preached repentance to all people, and they were of one heart and one mind, united in their belief, and there were no poor among them. When they gathered, people would bring what they had and divide it equally so that no one would be without. Then, due to their faithfulness, God would multiply it and give the increase. A few loaves of bread would turn into a few hundred, and a few fishes would turn into more than enough. Yahweh walked amongst them.

For years, they laid the foundations and built the walls—tall, thick walls made of stones from the mountains with massive wooden gates. The ramparts stretched for miles around the city, thirty to forty feet high, with towers even higher. It was a well-fortified city, a haven, a beacon of light, home to righteous people who loved God.

Years had passed, and Methuselah had grown to be a mighty warrior. However, much like his father, he had a heart for God and prayed daily that his life would glorify God. One day, he was visited by the archangel Gabriel, who gave him a heavenly instrument. When Methuselah held it in his hand, it was as bright as the sun. It was a sword that could slay demons, giants, and monsters. Methuselah told his father Enoch what had happened and showed him the sword. Enoch fell to the ground and prayed to God to watch over and protect his son. Enoch knew that God was preparing his son for a higher purpose.

Defend the City of Enoch

As Enoch's city flourished on Mount Hermon, a dark and terrifying force marched towards it. Azazel, one of the leaders of the Fallen Angels, the Watchers, left Egypt to lead this unholy army to overcome this bright shining city on a hill. He brought with him the remains of the fallen angels, with glowing eyes and swords. They flew above, their spiritual bodies glowing with an eerie light. Demons swarmed around the city's walls like dark locusts, making horrific, ear-piercing screams. They also had giants towering over ten feet tall, with skin as thick as elephants, making them invulnerable to arrows and spears.

He brought with them flying monsters called Ziz, giant birdlike creatures with wings that spanned over ten feet, and the Behemoth, a giant rhino. The evil men of the Canaanites, numbering in the thousands, had come to make war as well. Dark skies followed them; the sun was hidden by clouds. Azazel's camp reeked of blood, smoke, and defilement. Giants would devour the weak, and women's anguished screams pierced the air as incubi claimed them. Lilith, Azazel's wife, presented an infant for sacrifice, its mother's dead eyes staring into the cold, dark night while hellhounds fought over her still-twitching limbs.

The dark forces were at Enoch's gate; Enoch gazed out at the hellish sea encamped outside his city. His knees buckled, sending him to the floor. "Father, if thou be willing, lift this darkness from my people; nevertheless, not my will, but Thine, be done." Enoch knew that this was more than just a battle of good versus evil; it was even more spiritual than that. All that he had ever learned and taught about God was going to be tested, for he was defending against forces that nobody would have conceived. The outlook was very grim.

Azazel, the leader of the fallen Watchers, was shouting, "We will destroy this righteous remnant and rule the ancient world!" They brought the siege engines and the massive catapults to make war. As they inched closer, fear grew. Methuselah approached his father with fear and wonder. "Son," Enoch said, "the time has come. Go get your sword!"

As Enoch stood in one of the watchtowers, he addressed his people, perhaps for the last time. "My brothers, fathers, sons, and beloved people of Zion! This evil has come upon us and Heaven itself. Our faith has been a beacon for the lost, and evil has trembled. Out there are fallen ones, once angels of light. Now they scream in torment because they fear our God is with us! Those giants and creatures are mere flesh and blood and will fall by the sword. We have battled evil before and have been victorious, and we will again! For we are not fighting for land or riches but for the very soul of man! Shall we let darkness consume all that is good? No, I say! So let our hearts be filled with Holy Spirit and fire! Let our swords be wielded with righteous anger! For Zion! For God! Shall we stand strong? Shall we STAND STRONG!!"

Then suddenly, a ray of light broke through, and Enoch could hear Yahweh's voice.

God spoke to Enoch: "Open your mouth and speak, and every word of your mouth will be fulfilled against Azazel and all his company." Enoch obeyed, proclaiming in a loud, thundering voice: "Glory be to Yahweh, the Lord God of Heaven and Earth! I condemn you, Azazel, and your army!"

Suddenly, angels loyal to God descended from Heaven, fighting against Azazel's army. The ground shook, causing the Nephilim giants to stumble and fall. The wicked men grew faint of heart and fled in terror as God's judgment fell upon them. The terror birds crashed to the earth, their giant wings broken. The giant Behemoth recoiled, injured by heavenly forces. The demons of Mastema fled in terror, abandoning the fight. Fallen angels, including the other leader Shamhazai, were captured or killed. The fallen Watcher Azazel himself was captured and bound by the archangel Raphael. The rest of the dark forces retreated in disarray.

The battle was won; however, the war was not over. The dark forces regrouped in the valley of Danak near Enoch's city. Azazel's replacement, a fallen angel named Marut, rallied the forces. They were determined to overcome good with evil and rule the ancient world. The Nephilim giants recovered from their wounds and were seeking revenge. The fallen angels who escaped capture rejoined the battle; the demons of Mastema returned, bringing darkness and fear. Marut led the counterattack against Enoch's city, seeking to destroy the righteous and claim the earth for darkness. Enoch and his people prepared to defend their city once more.

This time, Enoch gathered all the people together in the city square and led them in prayer. They began to worship God in Spirit and in Truth, proclaiming that He was the one true God and that all others would have to bow before Him. They proclaimed how great His word is, and that at the mention of His name, the enemy was defeated. Then they asked for the Helper to come, and all of a sudden the wind started to howl. The winds swirled, and the Holy Ghost fell upon them all.

Now they shouted, danced, and spoke in other tongues. They were all baptized with the Holy Ghost and with fire. They were all branded instantly with the mark of God—the Trinity Knot—which stands for the Trinity of the Father, the Son, and the Holy Ghost. Then, all filled with the Holy Ghost, they ran out of the gates that protected them, out to meet the enemy.

"You come to us with a spear and a sword, but we come against you in the name of the Lord!" shouted Enoch as they charged the enemy from the gate. Enoch's people fought bravely, trusting in God's strength. Heavenly angels helped turn the tide of the battle, striking down giants and fallen angels. Marut, the fallen angel leader, was captured by Enoch himself. The Nephilim giants fled, being chased by Enoch's warriors, and the remaining fallen angels and demons were cast out far away. Methuselah used his sword as a mighty warrior and brought honor to God that day. In his life, he slayed over 900 demons.

Enoch's city celebrated another great victory, praising God for His protection and His strength during the fight. The word went out about how God favored the city, and how brave and righteous were its people, and how they defeated giants, monsters, fallen angels, and demons too. As news spread far and wide, people rejoiced, and hope was reignited across the lands.

Celebrate Good Times

Time of celebration, people were rejoicing and dancing in Enoch's city square. Tables were filled with food, and wine flowed like a river. Laughter and cheering echoed off the city walls. Enoch smiled, watching his people celebrate their hard-won peace.

"Just in life, peace sometimes can only come after a fight," said Adam. "That fight could be physical, mental, or even spiritual, but peace and joy will come in the morning."

While the city celebrated, a bright light appeared in the sky, accompanied by a strong wind, making a mess of the party. A massive ship descended, casting a long shadow on the square. The ship's surface glowed, and it bore the symbol of Yahweh. A Trinity Knot was on its door. It landed softly on the square, and the door opened. Enoch approached cautiously, as if called by the ship itself. A ramp extended, inviting him aboard.

He looked back at his people, smiled, and waved, then stepped onto the ramp. It then retracted, closing the door behind him. The ship rose slowly, drawing the cheers of the city, and then it darted up like a shooting star. It pierced the clouds, leaving a glowing trail behind it. Enoch's people shielded their eyes, watching in awe as the ship disappeared into the heavens.

Enoch stood inside, hesitant to take another step. Then he heard a gentle voice saying, "Enoch, highly favored servant of Yahweh, come witness the heavenly realms and the glory of God." The ship soared through the clouds into pure blue filament and then darkness, with specks of light scattered about. As he looked back, he could see the place where he came from as a giant ball growing smaller. Suddenly, a soft glow emanated from the ship's interior walls, illuminating a corridor of pearl-white panels, and under his feet was a river of gold leading to a large circular door with colorful and intricate symbols.

Enoch walked cautiously to the door, and as he approached, the door opened and struck him down with the brightest of lights, as if he had been asleep and opened his eyes to the brilliance of the sun. Gradually, Enoch was able to see God's great throne. He saw the Head of Days on the left side of God and the Ancient of Days on the right side of God. Enoch fell to his knees and covered his head.

"My Lord, my Lords, your humble servant asks forgiveness. I am so ashamed of my failures; forgive my iniquities. Holy, holy art thou, holy, holy, again I say holy." The Head of Days and the Ancient of Days looked upon Enoch with gentle eyes and a soft voice. "Enoch, faithful servant, your faithfulness is a cloak of honor that covers your head." Then they took Enoch's hands and led him through the doorway, and a brilliant light enveloped them.

The Ancient Angel said to Enoch, "This is the First Heaven above the clouds. This is part of the heavens where the angels are found. Also, the elders of the constellations live here, and it is where the morning dew and snow come from."

Then everything got dark. "Now this is the Second Heaven; it is a prison for the angels that rebelled. You see, they are hanging from chains as they wait for Judgment Day." Enoch could see Marut, the fallen Watcher that he had captured earlier, hanging from the chains.

"This, Enoch, is the Third Heaven. It is paradise, and it contains groves of orchards like you have never seen before, and this place is for the righteous who die before their time. This orchard has within it the Tree of Life."

"Now, on the northern section, it is reserved for the wicked. It is cold and frozen, and it has an endless river of fire flowing through it. This part is home to the fiercest angels, who torture the condemned sinners, such as murderers and those that would harm children.”

“Now, Enoch,” said the Ancient One, “this is the Fourth Heaven. It has twelve great gates on the sun’s surface, each with a path to the dark side of the moon. There are three thousand angels that live here. There are also creatures that have six wings; they play music and help the angels sing praises to the Lord.”

“Now, this next place is considered a place of immense sadness, Enoch. This is the Fifth Heaven. It is full of giant soldiers called the Grigori. These soldiers chose to serve Satan instead of God. Although the faces of all in the Fifth Heaven are withered, their souls still sing praises to God. It is punishment for the choices they made.”

“Now we have the Sixth Heaven. It is the home of the seven groups of angels that rule the stars and how they move. They also manage different kingdoms around the earth by keeping track of the good and the bad things men do.”

“Here we have the Seventh Heaven. This is the angelic realm, and it is filled with angels loyal to Yahweh.”

“This is the Eighth Heaven. This place controls the seasons year-round. It also houses the twelve starry constellations.”

“This is the Ninth Heaven; it has twelve mansions belonging to the stars.”

“Now we have come to the Tenth Heaven, the highest heaven. You see, there is the Throne that God will sit upon when He judges the souls of mankind. It sits empty for now, but soon, Enoch… very soon.”

Enochs Return Home

Then the Ancient Angel told Enoch that he had to tell his people all that he had seen and that he must write it down for future generations, and that it was time for him to depart. Enoch was transported back down to earth into the midst of his people, who were still celebrating. Immediately, they stopped in astonishment and asked him, "What did you see, and where did you go?"

"My brothers and sisters, you are not going to believe what I have seen." They were amazed and astonished. Enoch went on long into the night, telling them about everything. They had so many questions, so he wrote down all that he had seen and heard. The one thing that he knew for sure was that they were not alone in the universe.

The morning came way too early, but it was already afternoon. When Enoch opened his eyes, Yahweh was there, just smiling at him, saying, "My man, get dressed; it is time for you to go." So, Enoch got dressed and stepped outside, and all of his people were there. He went to the center square, and from nowhere a beam of light encased him. Enoch just smiled; he knew what was about to happen. Nearby were some of his closest friends. He nodded at them, "Keep the faith, my brothers; keep the faith."

Then his son Methuselah came running. "Father!" he exclaimed.

"I love you, son, and I'm very proud of you. Remember all that I taught you. I go to be with my Father," Enoch said. Then, all of a sudden, he started lifting off the ground, and joy and excitement came upon him. He waved bye to everyone as he was lifted higher, and then he was gone.

Methuselah

After Enoch ascended to heaven, his son Methuselah tried to walk in his father's footsteps and lead the great City of Zion, and the people accepted his leadership. When he turned 187 years old, he had his first son. His name was Lamech, who then had a son named Noah, and baby Noah was the apple of Methuselah's eye.

Little Noah's grandfather would always hold him and play with him, and when he got a couple of years older, he would tell him about the God that lived in the heavens and how His angels would protect them whenever they needed it. He would bounce little Noah on his knee and tell him about the dinosaurs that roamed the earth and flew in the skies. As Noah grew, so did the stories that his grandfather Methuselah would tell him. Eventually, he told him about his great-grandfather Enoch, and how he and his people built the City of Zion and how they used to call it the City of Enoch.

He would tell him how they fought against the fallen angels, giants, monsters, demons, and evil men of all sorts, and he would tell him how, with courage and faith, they won those battles. He would tell him how his grandfather walked with God and was the only one to ride in His chariot of fire, and how he was finally taken away in a beam of light, never to be seen again, living in the heavens with God. They say that he is up there, interceding for you and me.

Now, the City of Enoch was always under attack by giants or demons. As the depravity of man grew worse, so did the attacks on the bright city on a hill, which could not be hidden. It stood for righteousness, a place where a man could still come and receive peace and forgiveness, a place where God would still visit. Methuselah became a prophet of the Word and of the sword, and it is said that he had slain many giants and vanquished over nine hundred demons. Methuselah was known as the Warrior Prophet and grew old and wise, fulfilling Enoch's promise from God that He would not destroy man while Methuselah still lived.

Days turned into months, and months into years, and Methuselah, at 969 years old, lived to be the oldest man in history. His son Lamech became the Patriarch of the City of Zion.

Noah

Young Noah was becoming a man, and his days were filled with throwing a net into the water, fishing for that big catch. As he grew older, he became an accomplished skiff (fishing boat) builder. He enjoyed working with his hands and spending time out on Lake Chad. It was a beautiful place with crystal-clear waters and fish of all kinds, a peaceful place where a man could find some solitude and dream about the future. However, even being a patriarch, his father Lamech had many enemies, and one day he was brutally slain.

Leaving Noah to step in and lead his great-grandfather Enoch's people. Noah was a righteous man and a great leader. His kingdom flourished, and people began to call it the Land of Noah. During an outdoors evening worship by the lake, Noah was leading his people in singing.

And then he saw her—Naamah's eyes closed and hands raised, her spirit glowing with intense love for God. She had a radiant glow about her; she was a woman of much beauty with long black hair. Noah was mesmerized by her beauty and devotion. After worship, he approached her, introduced himself as Noah, and learned her name. "What brings you here?" Noah asked.

"I traveled from Bethel for spiritual guidance from the great teacher Lamech, and I saw the crowd and decided to join in worship; I hope that was okay?"

Noah responded, "Yes, it surely was. Naamah, will you walk with me down by the lake? I need to tell you something," Noah asked.

"Yes," she replied, and as they walked, their steps were guided by a full moon and a million stars reflecting off the water.

"I'm afraid that you're too late. My father Lamech has passed on; his life was taken from him a few months ago."

"Oh, I'm sorry. He was your father?" Naamah asked.

"Yes, I was his oldest son, and now it befalls upon me to carry on his work and his message of God's love and mercy."

"What do you mean?" Naamah asked.

"Well, you see, God formed us from the very dirt that we walk on. He then breathed life into us, and we became flesh. He did that so that He could watch us grow in Spirit and in Truth, and that is the way we must worship Him—in Spirit and in Truth. We cannot come to God in any false manner because God knows everything, and what He wants us to know is that He already knows. So when we come to Him, we must come with a broken and contrite heart and confess to Him everything, and then we can rejoice because His mercy has forgiven us and His grace is sufficient."

Naamah was impressed with his wisdom and drawn to him, as if it was no accident that brought her there at that place and that time. They began a courtship that developed into a relationship that lasted over six hundred years.

When Noah was five hundred years old, God came to him in the land of his grandfather, his father. God said unto Noah, "I intend to make an end of all that lives, for through men and the fallen angels and the giants and the monsters that are on the earth, the land is filled with violence, and I regret that which I have made. I will destroy all of them from the earth. Noah, you must build a boat of cypress wood for yourself and your household. Make rooms in it and cover it inside and outside with tar. You must build it four hundred and fifty feet long, seventy-five feet wide, and forty-five feet high. Make an opening around the top of the boat that is just eighteen inches high from the edge of the roof down. Put a door in the side of the boat. Make an upper, middle, and lower deck in it. I will bring a flood of water on the earth to destroy all living things that live under the sky, including everything that has the breath of life. Everything on earth will die. But I will make an agreement with you and your sons, your wife, and your sons' wives will all go into the boat. Also, you must bring into the boat two of every living thing, male and female. Keep them alive with you. Two of every kind of bird, animal, and creeping thing will come to you to be kept alive. Also, gather some of every kind of food for you and the animals."

Noah did everything that God commanded him to do.

Noah was somewhat overwhelmed at the task at hand and that God was going to destroy the earth. Everything that he knew and cared about would be gone. He went to his grandfather Methuselah and asked him what he could do. Methuselah told him that God was a righteous God and that He had endured the sins of men and His own angels due to the promise that He made to Enoch, that He would not destroy the earth while Methuselah lived. But Methuselah was getting old—eight hundred and sixty years old—and did not know how much longer he could draw breath. Noah was concerned for how many people would perish. The friendships that he had made with people he knew for years would die.

Noah started telling people to repent and turn from sin and be righteous-minded. He thought that maybe if he could get people to change, God would spare them. "The earth is going to be destroyed by a great flood," he would proclaim. But up until now, they had never seen it rain; the moisture came from the morning dew or the rivers or other bodies of water. It was hard to believe that the world was going to end.

Much like it is today, people go on with their day-to-day lives and do not consider the times. When the sacred letters says that nation shall rise against nation, and kingdom against kingdom, and there shall be famines, pestilences, and earthquakes in diverse places: Repent, for the Kingdom of Heaven is at hand.

Still, they mocked him. "How can it flood?" they would say, and laughed at him to scorn. So, Noah started building the ark, which was no small feat—four hundred and fifty feet long, seventy-five feet wide, and forty-five feet high. This was going to take serious labor. He then commissioned the timber harvesters to cut down the trees needed for the spine of the boat itself. By the time they were done, it would require around thirty thousand trees, cut and hewed into various shapes, sizes, and lengths.

Noah never gave up on the hope that he might be able to change some people, so he kept on preaching righteousness to them, that the End of Days was coming, but nobody would believe him. So he tried to delay the Lord as much as he could. It was a big job and very labor-intensive with just hand tools. Every day he would work on the ark, and every day he would talk to somebody about believing in God—to no avail. Perhaps God was right: the hearts of men had waxed cold, and His Spirit could no longer stride with man.

However, work continued on the boat, and eventually the ribs of the boat were done. This thing was enormous—four hundred and fifty feet long, seventy-five feet wide, and forty-five feet high. Years went by, all the way up to one hundred years, and Noah delayed God's judgment upon the earth. The boat was nearly finished, and Noah began preparing it. He gathered and stored all sorts of food for the animals as well as for his family. After one hundred years of telling people to repent, for the Kingdom of Heaven is at hand, nobody heeded his warnings, and sin abounded. "How could the dew on the ground flood us? How could we not escape such a thing?" they mocked and laughed.

The Rain

Noah, who was warned by an angel, set out to go visit his grandfather Methuselah, who was at the end of his life. Methuselah assured Noah that destruction was coming and reminded him of the promise that God made to his great-grandfather (that He would not destroy the earth while Methuselah lived). Then he gave thanks to God for His mercy and how it endured, and Methuselah took his last breath. He had lived nine hundred and sixty-nine years upon the earth. Noah buried him in the way that was accustomed for them and then went home.

Along the way, he heard stories of how the great City of Zion, all of its people, was gone in that very same hour that Methuselah passed on; the people of the City of Enoch had been taken.

Noah could feel a change in the air, that evil was set loose upon the people of the ancient world. Noah quickly returned home and told his family all that had happened, and they all agreed that time was running out. The next morning, there was a rustle in the air; birds, two of every kind, were coming to the ark. Noah instructed his sons to lower the door and make ready for the beasts. Soon, two of every kind of beast were making their way to the ark. Then, for the first time ever, a drop of water fell from the sky, and then another, and another, and then it was raining.

The people marveled because it was the first time that water fell from the sky, but surely this was not what Noah had been warning them about. The rain kept falling, and soon people's roofs began to leak water, and their pathways became mired with mud.

Yet the rain kept falling—the rain kept falling down, down. The people continued to laugh and sing and drink into the night, and the rain kept falling down. But when they woke up, they discovered streams of water flowing through their cities, wagons and possessions being swept away by the raging waters. Soon, people began to climb up onto their rooftops and into the tops of trees, and the rain kept falling down, down.

As Noah prayed, the time had come, and he instructed his sons to close the door. A large wave of water came and hit the ark, and it did move. Now you could hear the people screaming and begging for help. Instinctively, they made their way to the ark, knocking along the sides and the door, begging to come into the safety of the boat. But the door was closed, and the waters came higher and higher until the screams of help were silenced by the drowning of the flood.

The End